A Little Lie

Max Turner

Edited by Dr Sarah Boyd
Cover Design by Max Turner,
using photo by *CameraCraft* provided on
license by Shutterstock

CONTENT WARNINGS

Mentions of past family tragedy and parental death, mentions of past bullying and abuse, mentions of past societal upheaval, age difference romance, uncontrolled magic, closeted character, coming out, explicit sexual content, a smattering of angst and some sex magic. All wrapped up in a Christmas bow and a happy ending!

22ND DECEMBER

Club Uro was the smallest nightclub in Three Rivers City by a fair margin. As a result, it was comparatively quieter, less rowdy and with a more sedate clientele than the handful in the city that had primarily non-human customers.

Awen wondered if the chilled-out atmosphere came from the decor, an excellently rendered under-the-water theme to suit the river it was named after. It gave the place a sense of relaxation as conjured fish swam in the air overhead, their scales reflecting the dance lights like kinetic disco balls.

Usually, Awen found it strangely soothing for a nightclub. It was nice to be around people without having to truly interact unless he wanted to. It made him feel like he was part of society, even though that was questionable at best. So questionable that it really was odd how much he enjoyed this place.

Tonight though, coming here had been a mistake.

Awen had been feeling lonely and wanted that buzz of activity around him, perhaps find some company for the evening to take his mind off reality. But he had not accounted for how busy the club would be so close to Christmas – not a traditional holiday for his kind.

Too many people. Too loud.

Awen had been doing so well these days, trying to increase his exposure to people and become comfortable in a society he wasn't quite sure how to fit into, but this was too much of a leap.

Too noisy to be here, and yet he was too lonely

to be anywhere else. It was always harder to cope with the loneliness this time of year. Everyone had somebody. Family, friends, lovers, as was evident from the activities on the dancefloor. The main clientele was of sprite and pixie heritage, and those grinding together were emitting a very faint glow as their latent magic was sparked by their motion together.

He looked away.

Awen had a discomfort with Christmas that was near hatred. It didn't make sense to him that any of them celebrated it. It wasn't part of fae traditions. He understood why the humans celebrated it, but he still struggled to understand why fae folk had let it bleed into their lives. Though he was aware it was likely just his own difficulties given that it had been decades since the war between the Seelie and Unseelie Courts had inadvertently broken the barrier between the magical and mortal realms. Decades since their two worlds had been forced to learn to coexist as, day after day, magic grew weaker, and all of their kind had to adapt to a mortal way of life.

Awen felt the fizzle of static between his fingers, a reminder – like those fish swimming above their heads and the slight glow from the dancefloor – that not all magic was gone, even if it could no longer be controlled in the same way or grow to the same intensity. For the most part.

Christmas, he was sure, must make all of fae a little uneasy. A time when humans spoke of fairies and elves as though they were those creatures of lore and not their living, breathing neighbours? It was unsettling.

But, Awen had to admit, there was more to his negativity than the strangeness of this holiday; Christmas made him feel a little bitter about being alone. While humans celebrated family and connections; he spent all alone. He had spent it alone for as long as he could remember, and year after year, it had become harder to watch the human world celebrate it.

The truth was, he wasn't sure he'd ever really wanted anyone. He just resented the expectation that he should. He didn't need a family or friends.

Awen let out a heavy sigh and leaned against the bar, trying to buy his own lie.

The pixie serving behind the bar came over with a smile. "Usual, kid?"

It felt odd to Awen he'd been here enough that someone knew him, recognised him. Maybe he wasn't as anonymous as he'd thought. Having a bartender know his favourite drink sent a slight jolt of unexpected pleasure through him, but it wasn't the same as having people in his life who cared whether he lived or died. Who cared if he lost control and hurt someone, again.

Those intrusive thoughts stung, and Awen felt the sudden urge to just leave, be away from others and preclude the possibility for those sorts of relationships. He turned from the bar, intent on leaving, when his gaze was drawn back to the thrumming dancefloor and landed on the most beautiful man he had ever seen.

Older, perhaps nearly twice Awen's age, with neatly cropped black hair greying slightly at the temples. Clearly a sprite with that slight iridescence to his tawny skin.

A vision in a smart three-piece suit, out of place as that was in this club.

An intrigue worth staying for, Awen decided. He might be all alone in the world, but that didn't mean he had to be alone in his bed.

❄

Brock Trevanion hadn't been to this sort of place in more years than he cared to count.

He could remember when there weren't places like this for their kind. Before the humans had allowed it. He could remember when Three Rivers City was still called Truro, though he had been a young man at that time. Back when the war had ended, and with it, their world, changing everything forever; it had started in this city, the epicentre, and spread out through ley lines.

The memory was depressing, more so because it reminded him just how old he was. Too old to be in this place with his subordinates, he reasoned (perhaps belatedly, considering he was here, after all).

Going out at night like this was a rare thing for Brock. After a few promotions, he'd stopped being invited by colleagues to after-work functions and hadn't wanted to intrude. And, given that his life consisted almost solely of his work, he didn't exactly have a wealth of other friends he might socialise with.

On the whole, he preferred it that way; he had

never been great with people and was too long in the tooth to change his ways now. Moreover, he had no wish to be any less private than he already was, no wish to compromise. But sometimes, these things were unavoidable.

When Rose, the department's latest employee of a few months, had invited him out with the rest of the team, he had tried to decline. But she had insisted.

"It's Christmas. Come on," she had practically pouted. Her reassurance that her boyfriend was also meeting them all there had been amusing. As though he had any concerns that she was coming onto him.

Even so, he'd planned to say no. But sitting at his desk, realising this would be his last day at work until the Christmas break was over, he'd felt a sudden urge not to go home. Not to sit there alone, twiddling his thumbs over the next few days off – during which his only plan was to spend Christmas Day with his perpetually disappointed mother.

There could be worse company for this final evening before the depressive festive season. Rose might be new, but she was proving herself to be one of the best Peacekeepers in his department, and he liked her a great deal. She was sweet and charming, and he felt almost brotherly towards her, was already keen to mentor her. Her boyfriend Alfred was... an interesting fellow, but Brock tried to excuse the human his eccentricities. It couldn't be easy for them to be a mixed couple, and yet again, Brock was reminded of his age as he considered how it hadn't been all that long ago that the pixies, sprites, fairies and all others from their realm kept entirely to their own kinds.

It was different now, of course. Now, the division was between the mortals and the magical. And even that division had blurred. The mortal realm had changed them, and they were all more like humans now, physically as much as in any other way. The humans couldn't tell any of them apart, even if the fae could themselves still recognise a sprite as a sprite, a fairy as a fairy even though they had all been reformed into a human-like appearance when the realms merged.

It was all a very heavy line of thought, and Brock sighed inwardly at his complete inability to enjoy himself. As a distraction, he looked up, watching the fish overhead as he considered whether to bother taking the time for a real vacation in the summer for once. It might be nice to go fishing...

His thoughts slowly drifted to the magic being used to sustain the fish and if the club had the requisite licence for it. Which, of course, they must have or else he would already have been here with a warning notice.

Brock looked away and realised the rest of the team had disappeared onto the dancefloor. It seemed there was no avoiding it when Rose saw him watching and practically jogged over.

"Come on, boss!" she laughed, clearly tipsy, as she dragged him over to dance.

Though that didn't last long, thankfully.

One moment he was dancing – badly – with Rose, and the next, she was dancing with Alfred. Meanwhile, Brock tried not to look as awkward as he felt, dancing alone to unfamiliar music surrounded by many people half his age.

This wasn't as distracting from his lonely existence as Brock had thought it might be.

A couple of songs later, he drifted back to the edge of the dancefloor. He was on the verge of leaving, having decided that this was actually a terrible idea and would make him feel lonelier than ever and a fool to boot.

Then, looking aimlessly around the room trying to find something to focus on other than his own patheticness, Brock's gaze fell on the young man at the bar.

He was slight, though not quite willowy, with dark, curly hair that reached down to his shoulders and eyes even darker – particularly striking against his ivory skin. He had the androgynous characteristics of many pixies, but it was particularly enchanting on this young man.

And what was more, the boy seemed to be looking at him just as intently – to the extent that he appeared oblivious to the several other patrons at the bar who were practically begging for his attention.

There was something in that gaze that made Brock feel… good. Which was unusual for this time of year.

He hated Christmas; there was something about it that stripped him of his usual confidence and charm. It was hard to keep up that impression when sadness seeped into your bones the more you saw people enjoying the holiday cheer as couples. Harder to turn on that charm when he knew his own happiness was not an option. Instead, year after year, he had to endure his mother asking when he would finally settle down, knowing he'd never get up the nerve to tell her the truth of his inclinations.

Any other time of the year, he might not have felt this way, might have enjoyed the freedom and lack of compromise that came with being single. But Christmas? It had been the same since he turned twelve and understanding dawned that he was gay.

Lonely. Hopelessly so.

But that look! Brock felt warm and bolstered by it. That look made him want to stride over to the young man and talk to him, flirt with him. Take him home and—

And that's where he faltered.

It had been years since he had even remotely attempted flirting with someone, much less picking someone up. But those attempts faded to a distant memory as he looked into those dark pools drawing him in.

The boy turned on his stool, fully facing Brock now, and he could see he wore tight, dark jeans and a loose, blousy shirt that was open to his mid-chest, making Brock's mouth water and his blood pound.

He was halfway to the bar before he even realised he'd started walking.

Awen brightened as he saw the silver fox of a man start walking towards him from the edge of the dancefloor. He turned to the bar and ordered another drink, deciding that a bit of fun was exactly what he needed, an escape in every sense of the word.

His living situation was adequate, but the thought of spending the entirety of the Christmas holidays in that place? Awen shuddered. If he could find someone else's warm bed to sleep in just for tonight, it would be better than nothing.

The man, as predicted, arrived at his side and took the bar stool next to him. He cleared his throat before asking Awen, "Can I get you a drink?"

The words were crooned in a way that might have been considered charming a decade or two ago, but Awen could overlook the old-fashioned charm for such a fine-looking sprite. In fact, just the man being there grounded him somewhat. The residual magic in him was tantalising. Not as much magic as Awen had, of course, but enough that it was clear he must regularly use what little power he had. There was a sense of control there, of being able to wield the magic as it should be, as Awen struggled with.

The remaining flighty feelings Awen had felt began to recede. It was calming and reassuring. It felt like the rest of the room had disappeared, and he was grateful for it. It was so infrequent that he felt this way, grounded by someone's presence. And never to this degree before.

The pixie behind the bar set a glass down next to Awen and began to fill it with sweet beer. A human beverage made all the better by spices known only to the Seelie Court.

Awen pointed at the glass. "I've already got one, thanks. Can I get you a drink?"

The older man looked confused for a moment, and it was all Awen could do not to roll his eyes in disappointment. He had known men like this before. The type that had started to integrate into human society before humans ceded everything to the Seelie Court. The type that believed in those heteronormative ways like humans did. He was a man as much as a sprite, and he thought an effeminate pixie like Awen should be treated as human men often treated human women. He probably wasn't even into men, just drunk and experimenting before he got too old to get it up.

He shouldn't have ordered the new drink, after all, Awen thought with a sigh. "It's ok, don't worry about it. I'm not staying—" he started, picking up his glass with the intention of drinking it down and leaving the club.

But then, in a slight panic, the man answered quickly, "Yes, I'll have what you're having. Thank you."

Awen quirked a brow, grew a lopsided grin and signalled the bartender.

Brock was so out of his comfort zone it was troubling. It made him feel more vulnerable than he ever had in the field as a Peacekeeper. But then, it wasn't like he knew any incantations against this sort of assault, and he wasn't sure he wanted to.

And, of course, it wasn't actually an assault. It was… flirting.

Brock bit his lower lip as he set down his second

empty glass, both drinks bought by his young companion, whose fingers were now playing lightly over the back of Brock's hand.

They had been talking for an hour and said nothing of importance. General chit-chat, laughter and flirting. Personal information shared sparingly.

Until Awen, as the young man had introduced himself, said, "I think it so strange that we celebrate Christmas. I don't think I like it much. It's not part of our traditions."

Brock was taken aback by both the words and the candidness. Christmas was something that had, in some tangential ways, always been part of their world. Before the change, many a sprite or elf would cross to the mortal world and get jobs at that time of year, in Santa's grottos and other such places. Exploiting the season's fairy stories to spend time in the mortal realm and indulge their curiosity with little suspicion.

A curiosity about humans that many would now probably take back if it meant having the realms divided once more.

That the boy didn't understand this was surprising to Brock and begged the question, "Where did you grow up?"

Awen's eyes narrowed, and it was instantly clear Brock had hit a nerve as the pixie waved his hand dismissively and seemed to retreat into himself as though he had given away something he hadn't intended to. He was immediately guarded, and Brock felt a pang in his chest. He let the matter drop in favour of keeping the company.

"Shall I get us more drinks?" Brock asked

instead.

Awen studied him for a moment, and Brock was worried he was going to decline and leave. But instead, Awen grinned, leaned in and kissed him gently. He allowed his lips to part, and the boy continued his slow exploration until Brock felt breathless. There was a power there that Brock couldn't quite identify, a spark of magic between them unlike anything Brock had experienced before.

Finally, the boy pulled back and slowly fluttered his eyelashes.

"Or do you want to take me home?"

❄

Awen whistled as Brock ushered him into the luxurious apartment. The man had expensive tastes, and it suited him the way it often did those who had it and knew how to wear it well. Much like his three-piece suit in the nightclub, tailored to him perfectly. It should have been out of place. It had been out of place, but as soon as the sprite had started speaking, Awen's opinion changed. The suit was tailored to his personality as much as his body, Awen thought. Confident and fastidious, well-groomed in a way that spoke of how he expected to be perceived in the world. And, perhaps, a shield of sorts.

"I… don't usually do this sort of thing," Brock said as he closed the door behind them, sounding cautious rather than nervous.

Awen wasn't an idiot; he had recognised Brock's

name on introduction, as anyone likely would have. Though Awen had to admit to a special interest in knowing everything he could about the Department for Magical Management.

In fact, he had considered calling it a night when he realised the man flirting with him was a Peacekeeper. Surely the last person he should be socialising with after everything. But there was something about Brock Trevanion that made Awen willing to look past the reaction he might have if he knew the truth about Awen's past. Not that he planned on raising that subject.

Brock had a sort of soft underbelly. A vulnerability and loneliness that might have been hard for anyone else to see, and yet it was plain to Awen, perhaps because he felt much the same way. As they had talked and flirted, Brock seemed to relax, and Awen had enjoyed his company more than most he had gone home with.

"Would you like a drink?" Brock asked, loosening his tie. He had already hung up his coat and was reaching to help Awen out of his. The gesture was jarring; Awen often found touch difficult unless it was on his terms. But he allowed it as he shrugged out of the oversized coat and nodded.

"Just a glass of water would be fine."

Brock looked about to say something but obviously decided against it and disappeared off into what must be the kitchen. Awen, always curious, followed to find Brock pouring himself a whiskey, a chilled bottle of water already set on the side.

Awen silently watched from the door as Brock drank down the whiskey and poured another before pouring the water out into a glass with some ice.

When he turned with the drinks in hand, Brock startled, seeing Awen there watching him. "Damn! You... you're quiet."

Awen smiled and shrugged. "Force of habit." He took the glass of water from Brock and went back to the living room, smiling warmly at the lovely view he'd had of his back and shoulders. The shirt and vest were very becoming, and Awen couldn't wait to get him out of them.

Brock indicated the sofa and waited for Awen to stand in front of it before he dropped into the armchair opposite. Awen set down his glass and, ignoring the sofa, stepped in front of Brock and sank to his knees. He rested his hands on Brock's thighs, trailing fingers softly as he pushed the sprite's legs apart.

If Brock was going to be shy, then he would have to take the lead.

Brock drew a deep breath, and Awen felt a slight shudder as he started to run his hands further up firm thighs, on and on, until he was reaching for Brock's belt buckle.

"Stop," Brock said, snatching up Awen's hands. "That... that isn't why I brought you here."

Awen quirked a brow. "Really? Because everything up to this point, and your clearly hard cock, says otherwise."

Brock scrubbed a hand roughly over his face as he let Awen's hands fall back to his knees. "I know... And I want to... I just. I don't do this. I don't pick people up in bars, not that there's anything wrong with that. It just isn't something I've ever done. But I wanted to get to know you better. This feels weird."

"You're making it weird," Awen laughed and let himself drop back so that he was sitting cross-legged at Brock's feet, propped up with his hands behind him as he looked up at the strange man. "But it's okay, and you're entitled to change your mind. I was just... surprised."

"I'm sorry. I understand if you want to leave."

Awen's smile dropped, and he felt a chill go through him.

He really didn't want to return to the shelter tonight. It wasn't that it was a bad place; it wasn't as bad as anywhere he'd been in his childhood. It was just loud and busy and strange, and... not his. Nothing was ever his.

It was limbo and reminded him of what it was like when he lost control, the consequences he might face. Yet another reason he shouldn't have gone home with a Peacekeeper. But even this was better than that feeling of being between places. He hated it.

It had been a while since he had first admitted to himself that the reason he picked up men in bars and went home with them was to play make-believe. To pretend he had this, even if just for a night. A lie, just for the night.

Something secure.

A home and someone to love him. The man didn't even really matter.

Usually.

With Brock, it felt different. And Awen had a sense that the reason Brock couldn't go through with this was the same reason he so often did. That fear of being alone.

"Sure, I could leave," Awen replied, getting to his feet. "Though, I guess it's kind of late and dark. Maybe I could sleep on the sofa?"

Brock looked a little anguished, like he was reprimanding himself for being a terrible host, as he replied, "Of course, of course, you can. In fact, no... have my room. The spare room is made up for my mother, but you can have my room. I'll take the sofa."

"If you're sure?" Awen asked tentatively, trying to seem hesitant at least. He had no intention of leaving, whether he slept on the sofa or in the hallway for the night. He had already let himself believe he wouldn't be going back to the shelter tonight, and he didn't want to have to disappoint himself.

"Yes, yes." Brock nodded, knocking back his drink and then practically springing from the chair. "It's just through there. I'm going to take a shower. Let me know if you need anything."

Awen nodded and didn't ask whether it was to wash off the sweat of the day and the scent of the club or to provide a cold blast to quell his obvious desire.

❄

Brock let the cold water blast over him on the highest pressure setting it would manage.

What the hell had he been thinking, bringing this kid here?

He couldn't do this. He hadn't picked anyone up since he was in his twenties.

And his mother was coming for Christmas!

He had so much to get done at the weekend.

This was all such a ridiculous idea.

And yet...

This boy really was an intrigue. Brock had been with pixies before, back in his student days. But the connection with them had never felt like this, nor with fairies. And definitely not with other sprites.

He'd wondered at first if he had imagined it in the club. With the low lighting and alcohol, the magical fish above them, it might have just been a residual feeling from that atmosphere, from the magic itself. But no, it had been clear as soon as they were alone together that there was something different about Awen.

On the surface, he seemed no different than any other pixie, apart from his stunning beauty, which might have just been Brock's own bias. But there was a strangeness to the way the air moved between them. Brock had often felt something similar when apprehending those misusing magic, those who had enough of it to do so. But it wasn't exactly the same as that; it was understated. He had a sense of something just beneath the surface he couldn't quite make tangible.

Out of habit, Brock re-emerged into the living room in just a towel, immediately realising his error in not grabbing a robe or pyjamas as he ran into Awen coming from the kitchen with a fresh glass of water.

Brock swallowed hard as the boy gave him an almost-coy smile that was perhaps not as coy as it seemed.

"Thirsty," Awen said.

"What?" Brock blanched.

Awen grinned at the reaction. "I was thirsty. I'm going to bed now. But... look, if you want to join me at any point. I mean, we don't have to... do anything. Just if you... you know, want to spend the night together. Just spend it together in the same bed, nothing... um...."

As Awen spoke, his words seemed less and less certain, and he looked a little vulnerable, the coyness definitely no longer an act.

He looked lonely.

Brock could relate. Sometimes he just wanted someone there to hold and be held by. Sometimes he just wanted someone.

They said goodnight again, but two hours of sleepless gazing at the ceiling later, Brock crawled into bed behind Awen and curled his body around the warm and comforting form before him.

It felt as though he was encompassing pure magical energy in his arms, and his breath hitched.

Awen had been sleeping lightly when Brock entered the room quietly and then very gently climbed into the bed. He spooned up against Awen, and Awen couldn't help a sigh as he relaxed back into the warmth behind him at the same time as Brock's breath hitched.

"Sorry," Awen started, realising from Brock's reaction that this must have been some sort of mistake, but then Brock's arms tightened around him a little.

"Is... is this alright?" Brock asked, and Awen smiled, finding the man's hands with his own and pulling them up to his chest. He hummed his consent and started to drift off in Brock's arms.

Awen woke hours later with the glow of the winter sun trying to burst through the curtains and Brock's morning wood slotted perfectly against the crack of his ass. Reflexively, he stretched and sighed and pressed back against the hard length.

Brock must have woken then because his arms suddenly tightened around Awen and then stilled, rigid. Like he was just remembering why the hell someone was in his bed. He finally loosened up but then started to pull away.

Awen grabbed his retreating arms and pulled him back into the embrace.

"This doesn't bother me if it doesn't bother you," Awen said, releasing Brock so he could still retreat if he wanted to. He felt him relax a little and then nuzzle into his neck, which drew a contented sigh from Awen. "Just tell me when you want me to leave, okay?"

Awen felt Brock nod, but there was another minute of silence before Brock said, "This... is nice. I haven't had this in a long time. I'm sorry about last night, I sort of... I'm not good at this. I'm sorry I led you on. I didn't mean to, I didn't mean it to be a lead-on. I wanted... But... this is nice."

That made Awen smile. It felt good to bring someone a little comfort, and it was a comfort for him too. Maybe they could happily share this lie together?

"I used to find physical touch incredibly hard, but sometimes... it's comforting." Awen found himself revealing, his gut dropping as he said it. He wasn't sure if there was just something about Brock, or maybe he'd spoken because he was in that lonely haze of Christmas?

Or perhaps the sprite was able to wield his magic as Awen wished he could; he was a Peacekeeper, after all. He had to have some magic under his control to do his job, but Awen knew well that its use was restricted. A natural magic then, something sparking between them that humans might call instant attraction but wasn't as common among their kind as it once had been.

Not since the realms had merged.

Awen was a special case in that respect. One of the few born with the level of magic they'd all possessed before the end of the war. An anomaly, born with more magic than it was possible to control in this new, combined world. The mayhem caused in his infancy had resulted in the only solution seen as appropriate for these rare cases: he'd been sent to live in a human boarding school. Completely cut off from his own kind in an effort to keep the magic contained.

Awen shuddered at the memories. It hadn't worked, and for a while, Awen thought that he would never find any kind of freedom or happiness.

Then, when Awen had turned eighteen, he was

released into the world with no understanding or preparation of how to wield the magic that had once overwhelmed him. He had been reassured that his magic was gone now, or so much so that it didn't matter anymore. In reality, Awen knew the magic was still there. He had just been beaten so often in response to any sign of it that his self-preservation had overridden it. The memories of that, of those years of pain, were heavy, and they hurt. But, Awen reasoned, it was better than what had happened when his magic had been fully realised.

The harm it had caused. He had caused.

He shuddered, and Brock pulled him closer. "Are you okay?"

"Yeah," Awen dismissed. "I just... um, used to be in a different place, and it's weird to remember." He let out a breath. "Sorry, it's not your problem."

Brock made a low rumbling sound in his throat, and Awen smiled at the reprimand he could sense in it. They were quiet for a few more minutes, and then Brock asked, "Do you want breakfast?"

Brock watched Awen intently.

From his position cooking breakfast at the stove, Brock could see through the kitchen doorway into the living room, where Awen was picking over his bookcases with an awed expression. It was understandable; few were in a position to recover Unseelie texts, much less keep them. A perk of the job.

Awen started to pull one from the shelf but then stopped and looked back at Brock. "Can I?"

Brock smiled and nodded as he flipped the eggs. He was struck more by Awen's concern than his politeness. He had something about him, the sort of good manners that were beaten into a kid, as he had seen the humans do with their children.

The thought made Brock's jaw tighten.

Awen handled the book gently, taking it and tucking himself against the arm of the sofa to start reading.

"That one is quite ground-breaking in many respects," Brock babbled as he watched Awen's face come alive at the illustrations and knowledge before him – a history of the war between the courts that had caused the realms to merge. There was such a keen brightness to him, Brock wanted to bask in it. He found himself wanting to be able to make Awen light up like that. He had never made anyone glow that way and had never thought much of it but watching Awen... he wanted the boy to look at him with the wonder and excitement he looked at that book.

He was jealous of a damn book!

Brock swallowed hard and looked down at the eggs just in time to realise they were about to burn.

❄

Breakfast was wonderful. Or perhaps the food just tasted better because of the company.

Awen never had breakfast with hook-ups; at most, he would grab a shower before heading back to the shelter. And he knew he should probably do that now, but he found that, unlike most hook-ups, he didn't want to leave. Instead, Awen just waited to be asked. And that didn't happen either.

Their empty plates before them, they talked. Not as flirtatious as it had been, as Brock awkwardly tried for something more substantial. He was careful not to ask anything too personal, trying not to pry. The effort was amusing, and Awen knew Brock must be curious about him on a professional level, if nothing else. That was his job, after all, to be curious and investigate, and that was exactly the reason Awen shouldn't be here.

"Do you live with friends?" Brock asked gently, his latest attempt.

"Breakfast was good. I've never seen someone put chives with eggs before," Awen redirected. Brock nodded, a soft smile, but an expression of defeat made Awen worry this might all come to an end if he didn't give something of himself. With a sigh, he admitted, "I've lived in a shelter for the last few years."

Brock didn't reply, simply giving a comforting look since there was nothing else to say. Peace shelters for those displaced by the merging of the realms had been packed full at one point but now only housed those who had not settled well in the mortal realm for one reason or another. For Awen, it hadn't been his choice.

"I rarely have a breakfast like this at all," Awen smiled, lightening the mood. "It was very good."

Brock returned the smile, and Awen noticed the slight blush at the compliment.

It was so easy to move back to casual conversation, laughing together over nothing of significance as Awen teased Brock about how overdressed he'd been for the nightclub. Awen felt himself sinking into the comfort of Brock Trevanion's company. And Brock seemed to do the same, more relaxed than he had been since they got to the apartment. His cool exterior melting and standoffishness slowly ebbing.

Even so, Awen knew it was time to go. Breakfast was over; that would be the end of it.

But instead, as Brock cleared the plates, he nodded towards the sofa. "Go ahead and carry on reading if you like. I'll only be a few minutes."

Awen blinked and fidgeted for a moment at the unexpected invitation. Perhaps Brock was gathering his nerve and would try to have sex with him now? Perhaps if Awen did sleep with Brock, he might be invited to stay another night in this lovely, comfortable place with the charming, if slightly bumbling, sprite?

It was a terrible idea, and the longer Awen

stayed there, the worse of an idea it became; yet he found it difficult to resist the company he was enjoying so much.

When he had done the dishes, Brock came and took a seat in the armchair as he had the night before. He picked up a book of his own that had been set on the side table, a bookmark over halfway through. When it was clear Brock was making himself comfortable, Awen cleared his throat and broached the topic. "Just let me know when you want me to leave. Or we could... um, you know." He gestured with his head towards the bedroom.

Brock looked at Awen and then in the direction of the bedroom, a blush appearing high on his cheeks. "No," he said quickly and apparently more abruptly than he'd meant to, from the way he then held up his hands in placation. "I mean, of course, I find you attractive. But I don't want... It wouldn't feel right. But please, you're welcome to stay and read...."

When Brock trailed off, Awen allowed him the reprieve of a smile and a nod and then picked up the book again. They read in silence for as long as Brock apparently found appropriate before the sprite spoke again.

"I have many similar books, about the history of the war and several covering the merging of the realms, if you care to read them."

Awen blinked, unable to hide his eagerness for knowledge he'd never had access to in the human boarding school. In fact, few had access to some of these books, Awen knew. He had looked for them when he first went to the shelter, wanting to understand who he was and where he came from. But so many volumes were restricted, and more than once, the Overseer at the shelter had told him he shouldn't be looking for such things.

There was so much secrecy, even among their kind, and many topics were thought suitable only for oral inheritance, storytelling from one generation to the next rather than being written down.

"You have so many...."

"Perks of the job. I have the clearance to keep some of the more guarded texts," Brock explained, though there was no boast in it.

"Why are they restricted?" Awen asked, rising and going to the bookcase to look over some more of the volumes. He caught Brock's expression before turning and realised he had given more of himself away. Of course, he should already know why they were restricted.

Brock was silent for a moment, and Awen could feel himself being watched intently. There was that crackle in the air that felt like their magic reacting to each other.

It was intoxicating, this sensation. Awen supposed it was what magic could feel like if you were a normal pixie or sprite. He had only ever felt too much when he was out of control or too little when he was made to stifle it.

And stifle it he had; his reaction to Brock was beyond his control, something small and natural. The human term chemistry came to mind. In school, Awen had always assumed the humans meant literal chemistry, the endorphins released when one was attracted to another. But now he wasn't so sure. Perhaps it was the mortal version of magic?

As these thoughts ran through his mind, the niggling one behind them all was that it was time to leave before Brock knew enough about him to reject him, or worse.

Brock rose and walked over to where Awen stood, his body immediately behind Awen's, not caging him but enough to make Awen shiver at the hum between them as Brock started to pull a book here and there. Piling them into Awen's arms as Brock spoke.

"The war was over, the damage had been done. There was no separating from the mortal realm. And so, some books were restricted. Not suppressed, I don't think it could be called that. Simply, the Seelie Court felt that looking back on the war and how the barrier between the realms came to be broken would get in the way of focusing on moving forward. The humans said the Seelie Court was acting like a nanny state, as they call it. But many from our realm felt it was important to forget about recriminations, forgive all those in the war, whether they fought for the Seelie or the Unseelie, and live together in harmony. After all, we had to live with the humans now too."

When Brock finished, Awen turned and found him standing with a small pile.

"But you should already know all that, every family has those stories in their oral traditions," Brock urged, and Awen looked away, his cheeks burning and heart thumping.

But Brock said no more, just set the pile of

books next to the sofa and resumed his seat in the armchair. Awen knew he should be worried, but he simply felt grounded and peaceful once more.

Awen took his own seat and picked the first book back up, a thin volume entitled A History of The Court Wars.

He was onto the second book when he started to doze. It was slightly thicker, with images of what his kind must have looked like before their bodies were changed by the mortal realm into something more aesthetically human. And while it was interesting, he found the comfort of the soft sofa and Brock's quiet company lulled him.

Awen woke to Brock's gentle hand on his shoulder, hearing a thud as a book dropped from his lap to the floor. His eyes were immediately open and looking straight into those of the sprite crouched before him.

This was it, then. Time to go.

"Awen, would you like something to eat?" Brock asked gently.

Awen stretched and then noticed the blanket that had been tucked around him. He sat and pulled it around him a little, creating an instinctive barrier as he roused. "What time is it? Is it time I should go?"

"No, stay. It's gone lunchtime, nearly three. I thought I'd let you sleep, you clearly needed it. But—"

"I should go. I should get out of your way," Awen cut him off and started to try and get up, tangling in the blanket and knocking over the pile of books. "Shit. I'm sorry…."

Brock's smile was soft and warm. "It's fine.

You're welcome to stay. I made some sandwiches for lunch and left them in the kitchen. But I must run some errands, I won't be long…. You're, uh… welcome to stay," he repeated. "Go back to bed if you like… um, if you need the sleep?"

Awen felt foolish and slightly infected by Brock's strange timidness. He looked away. "It's, um… it's noisy where I live. Lots of people. Old building, creaking boards. And no day sleeping allowed. I didn't mean to…"

Brock smiled and shook his head dismissively. "It's fine. I had work to do, and you were a nice distraction when I allowed myself a glance."

Awen wasn't sure who blushed more at that.

Brock wondered if he would stop making a fool of himself in front of the boy any time soon. It didn't seem likely. Especially after he'd grabbed his things to head out while Awen tucked into a sandwich, stood at the kitchen counter and Brock…

Well, he'd kissed him.

He had just absentmindedly walked into the kitchen, pulling on his coat, said he would be back soon and then kissed Awen's cheek without thinking. He'd hurried out so fast after that, he forgot his hat and spent the whole trip consumed by the fact that Awen would undoubtedly be gone by the time he returned.

Brock wandered the shops in a daze, buying the food and drink and other festive items he needed for his mother's imminent visit. He was sure he'd forgotten several things, which he'd probably hear all about when she arrived Christmas Eve, but his mind was reeling too much to care. He found himself hurrying through the list, wanting to get home, hoping that Awen would still be there.

Though he had no reason to expect it.

Awen had said he lived in one of the shelters; not many of them were left now. Brock knew he could detour to the office and look up residential records, see which one Awen lived in. And more interestingly, why he lived in a shelter.

He shook the thought immediately from his mind. As tempting as it might be to sate his curiosity, he couldn't break the boy's trust by doing so. If Awen wanted to disclose his story, then he surely would, and in the meantime, Brock would enjoy as much of his company as Awen allowed.

When Brock struggled through his apartment door with his bags and set them in the kitchen, he noted quickly that Awen wasn't to be found. His heart sank, and he shook his head, cursing himself for a silly old fool. What had he expected? What had he thought was happening here? The kid had just wanted somewhere warm and quiet and comfortable to sleep for the night. Or, well, he likely had wanted more than that, more from Brock, but Brock hadn't given it to him, and surely the boy would find interest elsewhere very easily.

Brock felt a sourness in the pit of his stomach at the thought of Awen back in the nightclub that very evening, seeking another companion. He stared at the neatly wrapped plate containing the remaining sandwiches.

And then heard a splash.

He walked, quicker than he meant to, through to the bathroom and knocked gently. More panicked splashing followed, and then an apologetic voice called through the door. "Sorry, I didn't hear you come back.... Um, is this...? Sorry, I didn't know if this was okay."

Brock swallowed and pressed his forehead against the door. A relief he had never felt before in his life soaked through to his bones, and for a moment, it felt like he was drawing magic through the door.

He had never felt such a spark as this before. Controlling magic was his job, and unlike many of their kind, he experienced it daily and on varying scales. But he had always felt on the edge of that magic; it had always been very distinct from his own. An artificial magic that Peacekeepers had to use.

With Awen, it felt like there was a mingling of their own magic, which made it hard to tell where one of them ended and the other began. Brock tried hard not to believe it meant something, not if this was all to end very shortly.

"Of course, it's perfectly fine," Brock replied, his voice cracking as he struggled out the words. "Do you have everything you need?"

"Um, I could use a towel, I guess. I was just..." Awen let out a light chuckle that made Brock's heart race. "I didn't think that far ahead? I just saw the bath and, well, we don't have one where I live, just shared shower rooms."

"I'll fetch a towel," Brock told him, needing to

walk away. Their continued conversation and the headiness of their connection had Brock wondering what Awen might look like right now. Flushed from the warm water, wet and naked.

Brock hung up his coat and then rummaged in the closet for the fluffiest, softest towel he could find before returning to the door and knocking again. "Shall... I leave it out here?"

"Can you bring it in? I promise I'm decent. Plenty of bubbles!" There was humour in those words but no teasing.

Brock swallowed hard; the sound of his heart was thundering in his ears as he let himself into the bathroom.

Awen looked beautiful. His porcelain-pale skin was smooth and damp. His hair was darker for being wet, curls now inky tendrils. He was breathtaking.

Brock looked away and placed the towel on the side of the ornate, clawfoot tub. Purple-tinged bubbles covered the water and any further view of the boy.

"Can you hold it up? And maybe look away? Or don't. I don't mind," Awen chuckled, the sloshing of the water making clear that he was indeed about to stand up from the bubbles.

Awen spoke with that same certainty Brock had encountered in the club, and he liked it. He liked that Awen had that easy confidence around him when others so often found him stoic and intimidating.

Brock did as told and looked away as Awen stood in the bath and took the towel, wrapping it around his body. Before he could stop himself, Brock picked Awen up bridal style, intending to set him on the floor. But he paused, the spark of magic between them all the more conductive through the water.

Before Brock could put Awen down, the boy leaned in and kissed him. Soft and slow and oh so very sweet. It made Brock's legs go weak, and he wasn't sure how they didn't both end up falling back into the tub.

When Awen pulled back, he smiled gently at Brock. "I wanted to do that again before you kicked me out. I can clean up the bathroom before I go if you want me to?"

Brock shook his head and found himself saying without hesitation, "Would you like to stay for dinner? And help me with the decorations?"

Awen nodded as his smile grew.

❋

Awen felt so safe and comfortable in Brock's arms, he didn't want the man to set him down. So, as he was about to, Awen cried out, "Wait!"

Brock looked at him questioningly.

"Can you carry me? I mean, um, the floor is probably cold. I mean, no... I just... Can we...?" He let out a heavy sigh, not sure what he was trying to say other than please don't let me go.

Maybe Brock understood because he nodded, carried Awen through to the bedroom and set him on the bed before stepping back. Before he could step further away, Awen reached his arms out, letting the towel fall and pool around his waist.

"Wait... do you... Come here." He kept his arms outstretched and waiting.

Brock frowned. "You don't have to..." he told Awen. "We don't have to do anything. You can stay as long as you like. I like your company, you don't have to—"

"I want to," Awen replied. "I want you... I want you even more now than when I saw you in the club last night."

He saw Brock visibly shudder.

"But if you don't want... I don't want to make you uncomfortable."

"It's not that," Brock sighed, a frown slowly creasing his forehead. "I don't do this sort of thing. Am I being hustled? If you want to stay, you can, you don't have to seduce me for me to let you stay a while."

Awen could have been offended, but actually, he could understand Brock's point of view. Maybe it was a hustle, going home with guys so he could escape the shelter for one night. But he only ever went with guys he liked, and he liked Brock more than most, and more by the minute.

"I sometimes hook up with guys, so I don't have to go home," Awen admitted. "But only ever ones I have a genuine interest in. I liked you before you came over and started talking to me. And... Brock, you're old-fashioned and stern but so sweet and soft. I think I really like that about you. I really do want you, but I understand if you don't want me."

❄

When Awen said his name, Brock wanted to melt.

No one called him Brock. His family, horridly, called him Rocky – a childhood name he hadn't shed as he aged, nor had it aged well. At work, he was always Trevanion or Boss. In public, he was Mr Trevanion, Peacekeeper Trevanion. On Awen's lips his name felt like an incantation.

As he stepped towards Awen, the boy smiled brightly and let the towel fall completely away as he wriggled up the bed. Brock wasn't sure what to do now the situation had arisen, but Awen grabbed his tie and pulled it gently, guiding Brock forward until he was crawling over him.

Awen tugged the tie further and further until their lips met, and then he groaned into Brock. This kiss was hungrier than before, passionate, as Awen's naked and still-damp legs came up around him. Brock let some of his weight down, pressing Awen to the bed as he felt a hardness against his own rapidly filling cock.

"You're so beautiful," he muttered against Awen's mouth before kissing him again.

"Please…." Awen broke the kiss to make the plea as his hips sought friction for his cock. Brock pressed down against him, his own hardness trapped in fine cloth, not nearly enough for the boy's release. Even so, he ground their hips together, feeling Awen tremble as he did so.

There was a spark and then the spread of warmth. Awen's magic seemed to seep into Brock, and Brock felt his do the same, joining them together before their flesh had even fully met.

Brock groaned his frustration and reached between them, balancing on an elbow so he could unfasten his belt and trousers enough to free himself. He took them both in hand, but Awen winced, and he let go. This wasn't a good idea without lube, not straight from the bath. He muttered apologies and fumbled in the bedside drawer, his whole weight across Awen, who just... giggled.

The sound of enjoyment made Brock relax, and he moved back, lube in hand, squeezing enough in his palm to coat them both. Awen was smiling up at him, his expression turning to bliss as Brock coated lube up and down Awen's cock, stroking it slowly. He was soft and warm in Brock's hand, his cock long and thin and a shade darker than the rest of his pale skin. It was enough to make Brock's mouth water. He lubed his own cock before taking hold of them both again, certain he wouldn't last at all long.

What had been quick and almost frantic was now slow, teasing. He swiped his thumb over the head of Awen's cock on an upstroke, making the boy shiver and whimper, more heat radiating between them. Without easing off too much, Brock coaxed Awen to move with him as he moved to his side. Then they were face to face, with Brock stroking slowly between them. He couldn't help but be fixated by the pleasure written in Awen's expressions. Pleasure and joy and comfort, all of it radiating through his magic. Brock felt almost overwhelmed by the fact that the boy was letting him provide this.

Awen's eyes locked on his, and he ran a hand into Brock's hair, mussing it. His smile was beautiful, his hand trailing down to Brock's nape and pulling their faces closer until he was able to press their lips together. Awen's tongue sought his own, and they were kissing again.

Deeper this time, exploring and tasting.

Ever more passion seeped into it until it consumed them entirely, and both were fucking up into Brock's tight fist. Awen pulled back, panting; his pupils were dilated, and the hairs on Brock's arm stood on end as though there was static electricity in the air. Perhaps that was one way to describe the flow of their magic.

"Oh my god," Awen panted. "I've never felt... nng, this feels so good, you feel so good against me."

All Brock could do was bite his lower lip and nod that he understood. This was new for him too. Brock was always so guarded and used to controlling magic, yet Awen was pulling it from him with no effort at all. Joining it with his own until it formed something of a bubble around them.

"Unng, Brock... I'm going to... uhnnn."

Brock pumped them together, only slowing as he felt Awen stiffen and his cock pulse, then the hot come running over his hand. It was all he needed to push him over, his own climax pulling through him with a shudder.

Awen's gorgeous mouth was on his again. Kissing him deeply, nipping at his lips as his hands touched every part of Brock they could reach. Each touch spoke of something Brock had not at all expected but could now feel very clearly between their slowly fading connection. Adoration.

It was spellbinding.

❄

When Brock rolled onto his back, Awen took one look at his ruined clothes and was caught somewhere between amused and horrified. The suit was clearly expensive, and Brock was an important man; Awen could imagine him not being very happy with come stains on his suit, no matter how amusing.

The sprite must have caught his expression because he looked down and then smiled, gentle, and dismissive. "I have other suits." Brock's words came out as a soft, reassuring rumble that made Awen smile. He closed his eyes as Brock's hand snaked up into his now dry and dishevelled hair and pulled him in for another kiss.

"Did you feel it?" Brock asked as he let Awen pull back. "The magic?"

Awen frowned, unsure how to respond to the look of awe on Brock's face.

He had felt it; of course, he had. The way his magic had felt like it might move past his control yet never crossed that line. It wasn't like when things had gotten bad before; it felt measured. It had melded with Brock's magic and was going to do nothing more than that.

And it had felt... Awen trembled at the memory.

But didn't Brock always feel this? Awen had assumed, knowing that Brock must regularly use magic for his job, that this was to be expected between them.

Awen pulled away, not knowing what to say that would not end badly. It was clear Brock already suspected that Awen didn't fit in as he should. But if he knew the truth, what would he think? He was a Peacekeeper, after all. How could he keep company with someone like Awen? His very existence was the antithesis of Brock's duty.

"What is it?" Brock asked, clearly concerned as he sat up, moving closer to Awen.

Awen shook his head and smiled. "Nothing. I'm fine."

Brock clearly had questions but seemed to decide they could wait. Instead, he smiled and pulled Awen to him as he lay back down until Awen was straddling him in his soiled suit.

Awen laughed. "You're getting me all messy, I just had a bath!"

"I think you were already plenty messy." Brock trailed a finger down Awen's chest, finding the spots of come stuck to his skin and, further down, to the soft hair above his crotch.

Awen quivered at the touch.

"Should I stop?" Brock rasped.

He looked concerned again, and Awen knew Brock saw him as flighty. Not that he was wrong. Anyone else and Awen would have left by now, yet here he still was.

"Don't stop." Awen breathed the words and was pulled down into another soft kiss.

It was so tender it almost broke his heart.

Awen imagined this was what love would feel like. Soft, tender, passionate, amusing. This wasn't like the fumbles and half-drunken sex he'd had with others.

Awen's cock was already stirring again, and he felt a very physical desire for Brock to be naked too. He pulled at the already loosened tie, trying to avoid breaking the kiss. But Brock pushed him back until they parted again.

"Awen... Stay tonight. Please." It wasn't a command or a plea, it just was, and Awen felt the words pull everything within him tight and ready to uncoil.

"Yes."

❄

Brock had never known a time like this in his life. None of his short-lived flings had been like this, and on reflection, he wouldn't have wanted them to be.

It was a lie, of course, a fantasy, what they were doing. But neither of them could pull away from it. Instead, they allowed themselves another night of pretending they were something to each other, that this was their Christmas together.

Brock cooked them dinner while Awen unpacked the boxes Brock had pulled out from the closet in the spare room. They ate and talked casually, even as their feet found each other under the table, and they played footsie while neither acknowledged it.

After dinner, they unpacked the Christmas tree.

Awen made a face of mock repulsion as he handled the metal rods holding plastic pines. "This is something I will never understand. A fake tree?"

Awen shook his head.

"More cost-effective for most humans these days," Brock replied, though not defensively.

"Then what's your excuse?" Awen cocked his head and an eyebrow. "You have money, and you're not human. I would have thought all magical people would have a real tree if they were to have one at all."

Brock smiled and shook his head. "I do have money, but what I don't have is time or inclination. I only put these decorations up to humour my mother. If she didn't come every year for Christmas, I wouldn't bother at all."

Awen deflated a little at that. "That's kinda sad."

"I thought you didn't like Christmas," Brock teased back, taking the "branch" from Awen's hands.

Awen shrugged. "Doesn't mean I can't appreciate when trees are pretty."

"Let's see if we can make this one as pretty as you," Brock said without hesitation but quickly followed by a blush.

Awen smiled at that and started to sort through the decorations he had already unpacked, glass baubles and imitation candles, which he also huffed at, while Brock slotted the small tree together in the corner of the room.

It took no more than an hour before they were able to set the star on top of it and turn on the lights (which Awen refused to call "fairy lights"). But when it was done, they stood back, Brock's arm around Awen's waist as they admired it.

It was all too easy to believe this lie. That this

was their Christmas together and that it could be the first of many.

Through the night, they pleasured each other with lips and tongues, hands and fingers. Magic sizzling between them in a way that soon felt natural and inescapable. Something not to be feared, as Awen had often felt with his own magic.

While they both climaxed several times, Awen could feel that Brock was holding back. He wondered if, to Brock, penetration was something saved for a serious relationship, not enjoyed with someone practically a stranger. He didn't dwell on it, though, because as much as he was now craving the feel of Brock's hard cock inside him, he was also content with the tender affection he was being shown. Being showered with and immersed in. He woke for the second morning in a row in the embrace of a man who made him feel like he was exactly where he should be. That they both were.

Even if it was all a lie, it was a happy one.

"Morning," Brock rumbled into his ear as he stirred.

"Morning," Awen replied on a yawn before stretching against Brock.

Unlike the previous morning, Brock allowed their bodies to press together. A hand on Awen's bare hip pulled him back until they were flush against each other, spooning. Awen hummed his enjoyment.

"I could wake like this every morning," he chuckled.

"Me too," Brock growled as he nuzzled his neck.

They were both silent then, thoughtful.

Awen sank further into Brock, and he took the advantage, pulling on Brock's arms to wrap them around him and hold him close.

"I really like you," Awen muttered sleepily. It was an easy confession, despite being one he had never made before. Never felt before.

"I like you too," Brock replied, and there wasn't any hesitancy there, as Awen might have expected the day before. He felt a new level of comfort as keenly as the warm glow where their bodies met.

"At first, you were just attractive entertainment and a warm bed," Awen admitted teasingly. Chuckling when Brock huffed and lightly pinched his side. "But! But I could wake up like this every morning." He repeated the words with an added emphasis. He truly meant it.

Awen felt Brock's arms crush around him, feeling extreme comfort at the pressure.

"I would ask you to stay for Christmas…"—a hesitation and then— "I want to ask you to stay for Christmas…." Brock muttered the words as his lips grazed over the nape of Awen's neck.

"Why don't you?" Awen grinned as Brock moved to nuzzle into his hair.

"My mother arrives tonight and will be staying until Christmas night. A whole twenty-four hours with someone who spends seventy to eighty percent of her time being disappointed in me and pestering me about when I will settle down. I can't be a bachelor forever, apparently." Brock's tone betrayed no emotion, just matter of fact.

This was clearly something he was used to. Resigned to.

Awen pulled away so he could turn in Brock's arms, finally ending face to face and enjoying the smile he was graced with, returning one of his own.

"Brock... does your mother know you're gay?" Awen asked gently, something that perhaps explained some of that hesitation and guardedness.

Brock shrugged. "No. Maybe. I've never told her directly. But I haven't exactly hidden it. I thought she would just... know. She's my mother." He shook his head. "It doesn't matter. We only see each other at the holidays, birthdays, that kind of thing. My family was never one you might call... close."

Awen nodded his understanding despite actually having very little understanding of how families worked. He didn't realise a small sigh had escaped him until Brock frowned. He shook his head to dismiss it and then grinned at Brock.

"Ask me to stay for Christmas."

Brock's frown deepened as though not sure whether Awen was joking or not.

Awen wasn't sure either.

"I mean... it's one way to let your mother know."

"You... want me to come out to my mother by having you here? What? Posing as my boyfriend?" Brock sounded amused, though Awen couldn't work out if he was being laughed with or at.

"Well, when you put it that way, it sounds... weird...." Awen chuckled.

"It does. But I appreciate the offer. And it is pretty tempting," Brock agreed and then kissed him.

✳

Brock thought his chest might implode at any moment.

He was caught somewhere between trying to make the most of this day – knowing that his mother would be arriving around nine – and taking Awen up on his offer. Though he wasn't sure the boy had meant it. Or if he did, it was likely no more than a desire for another night in a comfortable bed and a misguided attempt at being helpful in return.

It was unimaginable that Awen could actually be interested in him for anything more. He was young and beautiful, a rare sort of beauty even for their kind. What could a man twice his age offer such a creature?

Even so, they had spent so much of the morning in bed that it had been hard to pull himself away to fix lunch and start preparing everything for the next day. It took an hour, and it was an hour during which he missed Awen's presence.

Awen was luxuriating in the bath again, and Brock didn't dare go to him because he was sure if he did, they would end up spending the whole day exploring each other's naked bodies in and out of the tub.

Just the thought had Brock near hard again.

He heard Awen move from the bathroom back to the bedroom, his footsteps so light, as though magic carried him. Given their intimate encounters, that was something Brock could well believe. He had never met anyone other than Peacekeepers who seemed to have such a strong magical resonance.

But with the Peacekeepers, it came from everyday use in the job, most of the time sparked by the artificial magic they were compelled to use. With this boy, there was more to it.

Awen didn't seem to even understand much about magic. Much less than an average pixie should, and yet it came so naturally to him. Brock found it intriguing, both personally and professionally. He had already thought back over years of cases, but he was sure he would have remembered ever encountering Awen in his line of work. Nonetheless, that was where his thoughts kept taking him.

He drew a blank every time, but Brock's gut told him Awen had to have been involved with Peacekeepers at some point. He had to be in the system. His magic was naturally too potent, too prominent for him to have gone unnoticed by the DMM.

And yet here they were.

And Brock had no desire to know Awen in any way other than as a lover.

He pushed those recurring thoughts aside. His errands were done for now. The food was prepared and ready to cook, so he was free again and found his feet carrying him down the hallway. Following Awen without hesitation but with a resolve not to let things get too out of hand. He needed to keep an eye on the time.

When Brock entered the bedroom, his breath caught.

Awen, who had spent their hours together alternating between the clothes he had been wearing

Friday night, a towel, Brock's robe and nudity, was wearing Brock's clothes.

He was too small for any of Brock's trousers but had apparently found some black silk pyjama bottoms that tied at the waist. The creamy skin of his upper body was almost completely hidden under an olive-green sweater that swam on him. It was pulled down to expose one delicious shoulder. The entire ensemble had been belted by a darker green necktie cinching in his waist and holding up the trousers, giving it a beautifully graceful look.

"Gods. I thought you looked beautiful before. H—how do you wear clothes and make them look like that?" Brock tripped over his own words as he crowded behind Awen and lowered his mouth to nuzzle gently along the exposed shoulder.

He felt Awen laughing in his arms, and his heart thundered in response.

"I'm used to making ill-fitting clothes look presentable. I've had a lot of hand-me-downs."

"You look amazing." Brock was truly awed by Awen's creative ingenuity.

The boy might still be something of a mystery to him, but there was something about his presence that was bright and warm and calming. Brock enjoyed the way Awen made him feel. He had never before thought himself a tender and soft person, yet now he melted against Awen, holding him close and never wanting to let go.

When Awen let out an encouraging hum, Brock kissed at his neck, his hands roaming all over, touching every part he could reach as his cock filled once more. Then his hands found the tie-belt and started to undo it.

"Hey, I only just got dressed! Finally!" Awen laughed his indignation, and Brock nipped his shoulder.

When the belt came away, the trousers immediately fell down. It was sort of comical, and they might have laughed had they not been panting and rocking against each other. Brock didn't doubt Awen was as hard as he was, but he confirmed it anyway by reaching his hand down and stroking slowly.

"Brock," Awen breathed. "Fuck me. Please... please."

Brock groaned and didn't even try to resist.

He had been hesitant. It was a big move for some, and he didn't want Awen to do it because he felt he should. He didn't want him to feel obligated in any way just because Brock had let him stay. And in turn, he didn't want to feel like he had pressured the boy.

When Awen had made clear his interest on that first night, it wasn't because he liked Brock. Of course, there was an attraction there, but Awen had simply been looking for a distraction. And Brock didn't want that.

He wanted to be wanted.

"I need you," Awen continued, moving his hips so that he rubbed back against Brock's crotch and rutted into his hand. "I want you so much."

Brock let out a shuddering breath. The desperate tone made the words an obvious truth. And that was all Brock needed to act, to know that Awen truly did desire him. Not just a bed for the night, not just sex, but Brock himself.

"Are you sure?" he asked, even as he was undoing his own trousers and stepping out of them.

"Very," Awen said firmly, climbing onto the bed, sweater still swamping him as he looked back over his bare shoulder. Brock groaned again and pulled off his t-shirt when Awen reached for the lube.

"Wait," Brock said, staying Awen's hand.

Awen's confused expression also held some hurt that Brock hated to think he had caused. He shook his head quickly, trying to dispel the misunderstanding that he might be reneging. "I could use magic..." Brock found himself offering. He shouldn't, he knew. But being around Awen made him want to explore where magic could take them.

Perhaps it was tempting fate, but he had both a professional and personal interest in the response.

Awen's expression melted into a cheeky grin. "Peacekeeper Trevanion, are you allowed to use magic outside of your duties?" There was a playfulness there that made Brock even harder.

"Perks of the job," Brock breathed. He cast the spell he had not had occasion to use for longer than he cared to admit, rubbing his fingers together until magic sparked between them, a blue glow that crackled.

"Disappointing," Awen playfully sulked. "I thought you were being naughty."

Brock grunted, his cock painfully hard as he manipulated the magic at his fingertips for a moment longer before he pressed them to Awen's ass. Then he took in a sharp breath, shocked as Awen cried out and arched off the bed.

The boy's body glowed blue for a moment, resonating with the underlying hue of skin colour no longer visible in this realm, the magic crackling all over his skin.

This wasn't supposed to happen. It should merely loosen and relax. Brock had used the spell before, on himself and on lovers in his early days at the DMM, but he had never seen such a reaction.

Scared of hurting Awen, Brock started to pull his hand away, but Awen cried out again and grabbed his wrist, holding him still. "Keep going, oh my stars...." Awen could barely get the words out as his eyes rolled back in his head.

Brock had seen it enough over their time together to know the expression Awen now wore was one of ecstasy. More intense than it had been previously but pleasure all the same.

The blue began to fade, all except waves of blue sparks that raced over Awen's skin, radiating from where Brock's fingers eased into him.

"Brock..." Awen moaned, moving against his fingers now.

Brock was dumbstruck, unsure how to proceed, as Awen writhed and groaned. He had expected the boy might be more responsive than most given the abundance of natural magic, but not whatever this was.

When Awen once more pressed down on him, fucking himself on Brock's fingers, he added another and began to meet Awen's thrusts.

"I have never..." Awen's voice was shaky, and

his eyes were damp.

"Is it too much?" Brock managed to growl out the words, his throat dry.

"No, no," Awen protested, shaking his head firmly and pressing down all the harder. "M'close…"

Awen's cock, blue magic crackling over it in waves, was hard and leaking against his taut belly. Brock was afraid to touch him anywhere but where they were already joined. Unsure what the results would be. So, he continued to move his fingers, curling them around until he found that point of absolute pleasure within the boy.

"BROCK!" Awen cried out and arched, his cock spurting as he did so. It created an arc, splattering Awen's chest as he continued to grind on Brock's fingers until every last drop of come had been expelled.

When Awen finally collapsed on the bed, his body was surrounded by a soft blue glow, pulsing as he breathed before slowly fading until all the magic had dissipated.

Brock carefully withdrew his fingers and swallowed, taken aback by what he had just witnessed. "I've never known magic like that…" he muttered.

He didn't miss the way concern, worry, passed over Awen's expression before it was replaced by a sated smile.

"I still want you to fuck me," the boy grinned.

❄

Awen moaned as he rolled on the bed and lowered himself onto his front. His cock was trapped beneath him, and he could still feel the ripples of pleasure and the tingle of magic over his skin.

It was like nothing he had ever felt before.

His magic had never worked like that, yet he knew instinctively it was his magic, at least partly. Combined with Brock's in a way that Awen had always feared would be volatile. But it wasn't; it felt contained and controlled. Safe.

Warm and beautiful.

And Awen wanted more of it. Over and over.

More of Brock.

He was momentarily struck by a feeling of guilt. He was still hiding so much of himself from this man, despite the connection he was sure he would feel with no one else. The thought that Brock might suspect the truth about him terrified Awen.

With distraction as much as pleasure in mind, Awen lifted his ass in invitation, letting out a little whimper that did the job of drawing Brock nearer. He was already moaning and writhing before Brock even laid a hand on him. And when he did, the spark was undeniable, even without the magic.

"Brock. Please." Awen only just kept the whine from his tone. He lowered himself flat to the bed, face buried in the pillow and hips jerking against the mattress of their own volition. The sweater gathered under his chest, feeling rough against his nipples and jolting shocks of pleasure through him.

When he felt the bed dip behind him, Awen wondered if he should arrange himself somewhat differently, perhaps shift onto his back or get up on his knees. But then Brock was behind him, half covering him as he gently shifted Awen's left leg up the bed, opening him up.

Awen let out a soft whimper, and his eyes rolled back in his head at the sheer pleasure of Brock sliding easily into him until their bodies were flush together. The pleasure was intense, so much more than anything he'd experienced before, and Brock was hardly even grazing his prostate. That sensation of pulsing waves of pleasure tingled over his goose-bumped flesh again.

"Is this magic?" Awen asked, feeling light with euphoria.

He felt Brock shake his head against him. "Not purposefully. Perhaps naturally. You have so much power...." Brock's words were reverential as he started to nuzzle at Awen's bare shoulder.

"It feels like magic," Awen panted as Brock began to move, sliding back and forth and making him feel so wonderfully full.

Brock rumbled words against his ear. "It's not just magic... It's a connection...."

Awen was unable to hold back another whimper at the words. The thought that Brock and he had such an intimate and unbreakable connection was a pleasure in itself.

"Brock, I need you to..." Awen moaned, pressing back to take more of Brock inside him, wanting to keep him there always.

Brock moved. His hips shifted in slow and gentle motions that Awen thought might eventually cause him to lose his mind to the bliss, but he didn't care. He had been mindless once before, but it had not felt like this.

Brock sank his weight against Awen's back, and they moved together, rocking on the bed until the covers were rumpled, Awen's sweater was shucked up as far as it could be, and the pillow he had been clutching had fallen to the floor.

It seemed to last forever. Awen felt like he was in an intoxicated haze and had no idea if it was minutes or hours that passed. He didn't care. He wanted this to last forever. He wanted to stay with Brock forever.

He never wanted to stop feeling the magic that was between them.

Brock's hands roamed over him, and his lips and tongue worked over Awen's neck and partially exposed shoulder. Awen didn't realise he was whimpering constantly until a hand rested on his hip, and Brock shifted. It was a small movement, one that lined him up perfectly with Awen's prostate before he picked up the pace. Not erratic, but no longer slow.

Deep, hard thrusts that felt like they would shatter him into a million pieces of pure pleasure made Awen huff and groan. His cock was still trapped between his stomach and the bed, his balls aching with his need to come again. But he didn't dare try to touch it; already, the friction against it was immeasurable, and after the passage of another unquantifiable amount of time, he felt his climax pooling deep within him.

"Brock." Awen practically sobbed the name, and Brock started to thrust a little faster in response. The pressure against Awen's prostate was almost too much, and he was on the verge of begging Brock to stop, but then it hit him.

Awen's whole body pulsed with a wave of pleasure that bordered almost on pain as every muscle contracted and sparks seemed to shoot through every nerve. He could feel as much as see how everything started to go blue once more. He felt his cock throb against his belly, dampening his skin and the covers beneath with come that had nowhere else to go. Every point of contact between their two bodies caused blue sparks to fizzle along their skin, enveloping them both.

Awen felt the effort it took for Brock to keep thrusting through his spasming muscles until he cried out too. Brock's hips juddered a few more thrusts as he spilled inside Awen before he went limp against Awen's back, panting and sweaty.

The blue pulses washed over them both, throbbing in time with Brock's release.

Slowly it faded, the room suddenly seeming much darker for the absence of the blue glow they had produced.

As Brock caught his breath, he went to pull away, but Awen snatched his hand and held him close, terrified in that moment to be alone. "Don't... just... stay here a while. Just..."

He didn't need to say any more; Brock spooned against him, not moving until long after he had softened within Awen and slipped out of him.

❄

Brock wasn't sure when he'd ever felt more

satisfied or content. Or terrified.

There was something purely magical about Awen that Brock knew he should be wary of; his job had taught him that. He should perhaps even feel fear.

But that wasn't what terrified him.

He was terrified that Awen would soon walk out of his apartment and Brock would never see him again.

Their connection was visceral, and Brock wasn't sure he wanted to go without it. He wasn't sure he could, and he desperately hoped that Awen felt the same way. Every moment had been pure bliss, including lying with Awen after intimate moments, both too exhausted and in need of the connection to rise and clean themselves up. They napped briefly around mid-morning before waking and enjoying each other and the magic that sparked between them again.

When they did rise from the bed to freshen up, it was mid-afternoon, and Brock knew he should send Awen on his way. But he was unable to voice those words. Instead, he asked, "Would you like some lunch? We seem to have missed it, and breakfast."

Awen grinned. The boy had settled the sweater back into place after it had fortunately ridden up enough to avoid any soiling, and the silk trousers and belt had been donned once more. Awen truly was the most beautiful thing Brock had ever seen, and the thought of him walking out was tearing him apart.

"I do have a bit of an appetite," Awen told him with a smile that fell somewhere between coy and suggestive. An expression that Brock would have said could not exist before that moment.

"Make yourself comfortable, and I'll fix us something shortly," Brock replied warmly before heading to the bathroom.

When he finished cleaning up and dressing, Awen was gone from the bedroom, and he returned to the living room to find Awen once more in his spot on the sofa. He was reading again, and before going to the kitchen, Brock smiled at how well Awen seemed to fit into his life.

He made them both a salad bowl and some rice, which Awen ate with gusto, but Brock found his own appetite a little lacking the closer they drew to Awen's imminent departure.

When they finished, Awen offered to do the dishes, but Brock refused, needing the time to himself to collect his thoughts and decide how to approach this. He could ask Awen for his number or even arrange another day and time to meet up after Christmas. But he still harboured a fear that, for Awen, this was all he wanted to offer, and once he was gone, it would be forever.

With Awen once more on the sofa when Brock returned, he didn't hesitate to sit at the other end this time and pull Awen to him. Awen went easily, stretching himself out like a cat with his head settled on Brock's thigh. His heart swelled as Awen let out a contented sigh and resumed reading.

He ran his fingers through Awen's hair, twisting curls around his pinkie and enjoying the way it relaxed his lover. At one point, Awen looked altogether too relaxed and blissed out and shot

Brock a stern glance.

"I'm trying to read," he admonished.

Brock couldn't help his lopsided grin. "My apologies. I hadn't realised."

Awen chuckled, and Brock's heart sank; he really should say goodbye soon. But it felt so wrong – Awen already seemed like part of the place. Once he left, Brock knew it would be like something vital had been removed from the apartment.

"Can I see you again?" he asked abruptly. Wanting "again" to be immediately after his mother left.

Awen looked up at him, eyes glowing and a soft smile on his lips. "I'd like that."

As soon as the words left his mouth, though, his face dropped.

"But… I don't know if it's a good idea. You're a good man, an important man. I'm… a mess. You shouldn't associate with someone like me." Awen sat up and placed the book on the pile next to the sofa that had grown steadily over the last two days. Before Brock could reach for him, he stood and walked towards the bedroom.

Brock followed and watched as Awen grabbed his clothes from the top of the dresser where he had settled them. "You're not a mess," Brock insisted.

Awen turned to look at him incredulously. "There's a lot you don't know about me."

"Why does it matter? We all are a mess in our own way," Brock replied emphatically, calming before he continued. "I'm almost forty years old and have never come out to my mother. Never formed any kind of relationship because I was either in the closet or too concerned with my career... or both. Now I'm here with you, and you're half my age and... I'm a mess."

"I'm twenty-four!" Awen refuted automatically, but his sad expression didn't change. "Our age difference is the last thing you should be concerned about," he said, forlorn, before letting out a mirthless laugh and moving to the bed, sinking down onto it, pulling one leg under him as he perched on the edge.

"And it's not the same, Brock. Age aside, if I'd met you five years ago, I would still have been interested, and I know you couldn't say the same of me. You could never have wanted the person I was then." The words seemed to fall out thoughtlessly because Awen looked immediately like he wanted to take them back.

"Please," Brock pleaded, sitting next to Awen and pulling him into his arms. "Tell me. I know there's something holding you back, and I didn't want to push. But... if it's what is coming between us, please tell me. I want to be able to face my enemies head-on."

Awen at least chuckled softly against his chest at that. They were silent a few moments before Awen pulled back and looked down at his lap as though he couldn't meet Brock's eyes.

"I'm so lost, Brock. I don't know anything about this world of yours, and yet I'm here and have nowhere else I can be because it's my world too, alien as it all is. I don't know how to be a pixie. I don't know anything other than—" He cut himself off as though scared of what he might say next.

"Tell me," Brock repeated, stroking a finger lightly along Awen's jaw.

Awen took in a deep breath and let it out slowly, his expression conflicted for a moment before it eased into one of concentration. Brock could imagine that, in his mind, Awen was sorting through painful memories.

"I was a quiet child at first. Too quiet, it turned out. I started to use magic to communicate when I was very young. My parents tried to stop me, but it's difficult to reason with a toddler, and so the authorities became involved."

"The DMM?" Brock frowned, trying to recall if he'd ever heard of such a thing (though it was likely before his time), but then Awen shook his head.

"No, the Seelie Court. I'm told they decided I was too young to fall into the DMM's jurisdiction. But I suspect they meant too powerful. They wanted me handled, reconditioned. I don't remember much except the pain; I was too young to—"

Brock pulled Awen back into his arms and clutched him tight, shaking almost as much as Awen as he tried to fathom what had happened to this poor young pixie.

"It was like how you train an animal, I suppose. They hurt me when I used magic until I made the connection and stopped. The thing I really remember was saying goodbye to my parents. I was about five by then, and they visited me often in the facility I'd been placed in. But they were so sad that day. They had been told I couldn't come home; the risk was too great. I had to go somewhere there was no magic. So, I was sent to a human boarding

61

school."

"I…" Brock had no words; all he could do was stroke a hand gently up and down Awen's back and press kisses into his hair. "I can't imagine."

"They weren't good people. Discipline was paramount, and any infraction resulted in a beating. At first, I thought all the children were subject to this same tyranny, but over time I realised it was just me. I've never been sure whether they just hated having a non-human there or the Seelie Court had ordered it. It came to a point where I physically couldn't use magic anymore, not with intention. I spent every day terrified I'd use it by accident, and sometimes I did. A small thing here or there, like reaching for a pencil and it coming to my hand without my even thinking about it. The punishments were worse when things like that happened.

"When I was seventeen, there was an incident. Some school bullies had me pinned down, and one of the teachers saw but simply stood there and watched. I lost control. All that magic bottled up, I exploded, almost literally."

Brock drew in a deep breath to try and calm his rising anger, but it was difficult thinking of what Awen had been through.

"No one died, thankfully. But they were all hurt, all burned to varying degrees." Awen pulled back then, remorse and sadness in his eyes, "I didn't mean to. Even as horrid as they were, I never meant to hurt anyone."

"I know." Brock nodded and cupped Awen's face in his hands. "I know. Believe me, it's my job to apprehend people misusing magic, causing harm.

I have an instinct for these things and…" Brock was about to say he knew he had nothing to fear from Awen, but that wasn't quite true. He had sensed something in their time together, but perhaps he had been blinded by his attraction to the boy?

He wasn't sure if it was his hesitation, or perhaps Awen read something in his expression that made him pull away, moving further across the bed. "I would never hurt anyone intentionally, but sometimes I can't control my magic, and that terrifies me. When we had sex, that was… it was so perfect, and I could feel my magic, and I felt in control of it for the first time. I loved it, but what if it isn't like that every time? What if I hurt you?"

Awen voiced Brock's fears, and Brock had no reply.

Hanging his head, Awen continued. "The Seelie Court took me back then, after that incident, to the same facility I'd been in as a child. I remembered the smell of it, it made me retch. This was a few months before I turned eighteen anyway, so they simply held me there, cut off from anyone and everyone aside from a few experts who came along to poke and prod me on occasion. When I turned eighteen, they declared me no longer their problem. They kicked me out, and I ended up in the shelter. I've been there ever since."

Awen stopped then, Brock's mind reeling to take it all in. He had to resist reaching out to offer comfort again as his heart so desperately wanted, knowing he had to let his head lead this.

"Your parents?" Brock asked gently.

"I asked before they sent me on my way, and I

was told they were dead. When I got to the shelter, I looked into it myself. I didn't trust anyone. But they were right. They had a car accident a few years ago." Awen choked out a bark of mirthless laughter. "Can you imagine something so mundane? And had I been with them, with all this power, if I had been able to control it, I could have—"

"No," Brock said sternly, frowning as he got off the bed, walked around to where Awen sat, and stood in front of him. "You can't think like that. Besides, that's not how magic works here. If your magic was as weak as everyone else's, you wouldn't have been able to save them anyway. You would have likely died as well."

"What about you?" Awen asked, his eyes glistening with tears. "You have magic, you use it every day."

Brock let out a heavy sigh and shook his head. "My magic, the magic of any Peacekeeper, is almost entirely artificial, and even that takes constant practice and a great deal of effort. Yes, we all have some natural talent, that's how you either end up a Peacekeeper or the prisoner of a Peacekeeper. But it's not like what you have, darling Awen. Not even close." Brock cupped Awen's face again, rubbing a thumb over his cheek where a tear had begun to trail down.

"Are you scared of me now? You need to arrest me?" Awen asked, sounding small.

Brock chuckled and shook his head. "Far from it. You've done nothing wrong. And you seem in control."

"I'm a liar." Awen shook his head, freeing

himself from Brock's hands.

"There's no lie in omitting your past. I can't tell you how honoured I am that you trusted me with—"

"I changed my name. I didn't want the Seelie Court to find me again. I didn't want them to decide I belonged in that facility forever."

Brock nodded his understanding and found himself not entirely surprised. Awen was more commonly a name for female pixies, but he hadn't questioned how beautifully it suited this young man. He wasn't going to ask what it was before; it didn't matter.

This was Awen.

"I don't blame you. But that doesn't make you a liar, Awen. It's who you are now. Who you know yourself to be."

Awen let out a little sob and turned away.

Brock sat down next to him on the edge of the bed so Awen had to look at him. "And I disagree," he started, gaining a curious look from Awen, "that I wouldn't have wanted to know you five years ago, age aside. You took a sad old man and made him happier than he has ever been in less than three days. You delight all those who talk to you. Don't you think I saw the way people looked at you in the club? How they wanted you? I was almost too scared to approach you myself, I thought you would laugh at me and reject me outright. You have this beautiful power that comes from a natural magic you will always have, even when it is crushed down. You're simply enchanting, and I can't imagine you have ever been anything else."

Awen's face brightened a little as Brock spoke,

and so he continued, taking hold of one of Awen's hands in his.

"Earlier when we..." Brock searched for the right term to describe what had been between them. "When we made love, that was you. That was your magic and the control you had over it."

A small smile was spreading across Awen's face, and Brock had to press a kiss to the corner of his lips before he continued. "I'm not scared of you, Awen. I'm just scared I might never see you again."

Awen took in a sharp breath and then let it out slowly. Brock could practically hear the boy's heart beating like a rabbit, and electricity sparked between them again.

Brock smiled and pulled back, light sparks flying as he did so. "This is you, Awen, and it's beautiful."

"But... What if I'm dangerous? What if I lose control again?" Awen insisted, and the fear that he might hurt Brock was painfully clear in his expression.

Brock shook his head and smiled, brushing some of Awen's hair behind one ear before leaning back in and kissing him. The sparks sizzled over their skin but caused no pain, nothing more than the sensation of effervescent water. "Darling boy, I have no doubt you are the most dangerous thing I have ever known. As a senior Peacekeeper in the DMM, it is arguably my duty to keep a close eye on you and ensure you pose no danger to society."

Awen's smile grew at the tease, even if there might be some truth in it. "Brock." He smiled around the name. "You are the most wonderful person I have ever met."

Brock laughed at that and started to lean in for what he was sure would be a rather passionate and hungry kiss.

But there was a knock at the door, and they both stilled.

❄

Brock looked over at the clock on the bedside.

"The time!" he exclaimed before jumping up from Awen and the bed and heading out to answer the increasingly impatient knocking.

Awen sat up and adjusted his clothes to be presentable once more. He had no idea how he should proceed. Climb out the window and down the fire escape? Hide somewhere? He knew either option would likely make a noise Brock would have to explain away. But wouldn't that be better than Brock's mother finding him here?

He could wait, he decided. Sit in Brock's room until she went to the bathroom or to bed, and then leave quietly. If only he had brought a book to read while he waited.

He would miss the books. Being able to just sit around and read and not feel like he was in the way or should be doing something more useful. Being able to sit and read without the commotion of other people living practically on top of each other.

He would miss that he could still feel Brock around even while he was consumed with reading. He would miss his smell and his warmth. He would miss this home but only because of Brock. Even with all the books and the soft bed, and the ridiculously luxurious bathtub, this apartment would hold no interest without Brock Trevanion in it.

Maybe in part, it was the age difference or the man's position. Awen had lost count of the hook-ups he'd had and never felt anything, but this was a man he felt could handle him, and there was a sense of security in that and his settled life that Awen had never had. Perhaps that was something many men could have offered him, but they wouldn't be Brock, and together Brock was that whole package. But Awen didn't know how to be anything other than alone.

He could hear Brock and his mother chattering easily, though he couldn't quite make out the words. Although Brock had said they weren't close, she was still his mother. Awen could only imagine what that would be like, that sort of familial connection.

He shrank a little at the thought.

The boarding school had purported itself as a family of sorts. Not that he had ever been included in that. An outcast, unwanted. And looking back, he couldn't entirely blame the humans for that. Their world had been irrevocably changed by a war they took no part in. Their realm had been merged with another, which now held most of the power even if it enforced human law on all.

Even if the Seelie Court hadn't ordered the school to provide beatings and not discourage bullies, he could understand why the humans would treat him in such a way. The resentment, perhaps even fear.

Awen shuddered at the thought because despite understanding that fear, none of it was really

Awen's fault. He couldn't help who he was born to be.

If Brock had been distant from his mother all these years because of one thing he feared telling her, then Awen was sorry for them. It was so awful to live with the fear that you might destroy a family by being yourself.

Awen had never even had that chance.

He stood and brushed down his clothes – Brock's clothes – making sure he looked presentable. He went to the vanity and fluffed his hair a little to try and make it look slightly less like they had been fucking for near two days straight. Then he took a breath and squared his shoulders.

❄

Brock felt like his heart stopped when he heard the bedroom door open.

He hadn't been certain what he was going to do with Awen now that his mother was here, but this was not an option he had seriously considered despite their earlier joking.

His mother didn't notice at first, babbling about how awful the train was once you hit Three Rivers City, especially so close to Christmas.

She didn't notice anything until she did.

And Brock knew she did because her attention snapped to something over his shoulder, and she went completely silent.

"Rocky?" she finally asked, clearly having to make an effort to draw her eyes from Awen back to her son. His heart was pounding, and his palms were sweating. He tried to believe that he didn't fear anything. He wasn't even remotely scared of a lover who had been born with so much magic he could have easily turned into one of Brock's biggest arrests. But he did fear breaking his mother's heart.

"Uhm... uh..." he stuttered, feeling the sting of tears in his eyes.

And then Awen was next to him, looping an arm through his. He didn't need to look at him full-on to see that Awen was beaming a wonderful and welcoming smile at his mother, whose eyes now darted between them both.

"Rocky?" she asked again, her expression unreadable.

"It's so good to meet you, Mrs Trevanion." Awen let go of Brock and stepped another pace forward, taking her hand with no argument and shaking it fondly. "I'm Awen—"

"My boyfriend," Brock blurted.

He didn't know where the words came from at first, and when he realised he had said them, he felt sick.

CHRISTMAS DAY

"So precious," Brock heard his mother coo over Awen and blinked.

This situation was... not as he had expected.

When his mother arrived, and he had dropped the bombshell that he had a boyfriend, that he was gay, her face crumpled. His heart had sunk with more pain than he knew how to deal with. She had wept into her hands for a few moments while he and Awen remained completely still and equally unsure.

Then, when she finally looked up, dropping her hands, Brock had seen that she was smiling. "Oh, Rocky." She shook her head, and happy tears rolled freely down her cheeks. "Finally!"

She had turned to Awen and enveloped him into a warm hug, muttering something about him having finally made an honest man of her son, and how long she had waited for him to trust her with this part of himself, and please do call her Merryn.

When she had finally let Awen go, she turned the same aggressive hug on Brock, crying against his shoulder as she repeated over and over, "I'm so glad you're happy."

He had looked over at Awen, a wide smile growing on the boy's face. And even so, Awen had pointed towards the door and mouthed through his smile, "Should I go?"

Clearly joking. Or at least Brock hoped so.

Brock had shaken his head sternly and frowned until Awen was giggling silently, his whole body shaking. He had narrowed his eyes at the boy, which only made his body shake more with the silent laughter.

The rest of the evening had been spent with his mother in the very best of moods as she unpacked gifts for him and reprimanded Brock for not having told her about Awen. She would have brought him a gift had she known.

Brock was... bewildered but happy.

When his mother had retired to the spare room for the evening, Brock couldn't help but scoop Awen up against him and kiss him, hard. He wasn't about to do much more with his mother in the next room, but he'd been happy to kiss the boy stupid in his bed until they drifted off to sleep.

And now Christmas Day had dawned, and his mother was fussing over Awen as he did little more than exist.

Well, Brock could understand that; Awen was, in every way, enchanting. Literally. And if his mother was completely besotted with him, Brock knew he certainly was too.

They hadn't spoken about it, but there seemed to have been a silent realisation between them that they had to keep up this ruse. It would be unfair to explain to his mother that they had, in fact, only met days earlier as a hook-up. She was so thrilled that this tension between them, through which she'd tried painfully hard to support Brock without pushing, had been lifted. She was happy the truth was out and they could be happy in each other's company with no awkwardness as there had been in the past.

And Brock was enjoying it too. He hadn't felt this close to his mother since he was a child.

The happiness was only marred by his concern for Awen and what he had revealed about his own family. But as he watched Awen with his mother, he wondered if this could be a family for him. If Brock could be his family.

The thought was both terrifying and thrilling. They had known each other for mere days, and yet there was an undeniable connection there. One that made it hard to even consider saying goodbye.

Brock turned away from them and to the kitchen as his mother continued to gush over Awen's choice of outfit for the day. The resourceful boy had found yet another combination in Brock's wardrobe and made it his own. Today he wore a pair of beige linen trousers that Brock had found occasion to wear on a summer trip to Penzance, paired with a plain white t-shirt once again nipped in at the waist. This time, the white scarf from Brock's tuxedo for formal work occasions served as the belt.

Awen was a Christmas vision, and the sight of him made Brock's mouth water and his heart ache.

"Need help?" He heard Awen's voice close to his ear as he came up behind, snaked his arms around Brock's waist and settled his head on Brock's shoulder.

Brock shook his head. "All under control," he said, checking on the turkey that was currently roasting in the too-infrequently used oven.

He remembered how Awen's eyes had lit up when Brock started to prepare the meal. Leaving Brock to wonder exactly what Awen subsided on at the shelter. Did they feed him? Did he have somewhere to cook for himself? Brock was unsure of the arrangements but once again felt the overwhelming desire to keep Awen there with him, well-fed and happy.

Brock turned in Awen's embrace, overwhelmed with the thought of him leaving, and kissed him softly. He could feel Awen's lips curl into a smile against his own.

"Ah, the honeymoon period continues. You really should have a wedding before one of those," Brock's mother said from the kitchen doorway, making them jump apart. She looked at them with a knowing grin. "Oh, I don't mind it. You just both go ahead and be happy."

The moment of joy that Brock felt at her love and acceptance turned to a sour guilt in the pit of his stomach. He was glad she'd turned back into the living room and didn't see the expression on his face that Awen clearly did.

"Are you ok?" Awen asked. "Is... is this too much? I can leave... I can say I have another dinner to get to?"

Brock shook his head before even considering the offer. His desire for Awen to stay outweighed the guilt of lying to his mother. He pulled Awen close and spoke quietly in his ear. "She's so happy. I never thought... I don't want to ruin this. I feel terrible about lying to her."

Awen squeezed him. "It's only a little lie."

The words were meant to reassure but left Brock considering what Awen meant. Which part of this was little? This all seemed so vast and wonderful; he hoped it would never end.

❄

Awen couldn't help but keep looking over at Brock as he served dinner and the three of them tucked in. He couldn't imagine how guilty Brock must feel over the situation.

Well, perhaps he could if it was anything like the guilt Awen felt for not giving Brock a choice in this ruse before he'd burst out of the bedroom and outed the man. It had not been his place to do that. He wondered if Brock would ever forgive him.

Perhaps when his mother left, he would shout at him, call him worthless, throw him out. Awen was sure, at least, that he wouldn't take a belt to him as the teachers had so many times. His only consolation was that they had spent a wonderful weekend together, the memory of which he would always treasure.

He didn't expect for one moment for Brock to stand by the lovely things he had said over the last few days. That was too distant a dream to ever be reality.

Brock might have meant them then, but probably not after Awen had forced him into playing house in front of his mother like this. Revealing something he had no right to reveal and making him lie to her.

Awen knew he was dangerous, that he had the ability to ruin lives, but he had never thought it would manifest in this way. He might as well be uncontrollable for the havoc this had wreaked for Brock.

"Are you spending time with your family over Christmas?" Awen heard Mrs Trevanion ask and then realised after a moment she was obviously talking to him. He shook his head and looked down at his plate as he tried to regain control of his expression, shuttling between painful memories. Before he could answer, he felt Brock's hand come around his and squeeze.

"Awen is an orphan, Mother," Brock said gently, quietly and with reverence.

"Oh, I am so sorry," Mrs Trevanion replied in the exact same tone.

Awen looked up to find her expression was less one of pity and more one of unconditional love. Like one might give an abandoned puppy. Which was at least better than pity.

He looked at Brock, whose own smile was... loving. Just so full of affection and warmth. Awen could almost feel Brock's desire to protect and care for him radiating from him. For a moment, there was a crackle, just a hint of it. An almost imperceptible flicker of blue sparks between them for a fraction of a second.

"I... I need the bathroom," Awen said, overwhelmed as he slipped his hand from Brock's and excused himself.

❄

Brock had been on the verge of looking for Awen after a few minutes, but his mother had stopped him.

"Poor boy, give him his space," she said softly, taking Brock's hand and giving him a meaningful look. "You must mean so much to him that he has put himself in a potentially painful situation." His mother's tone was sympathetic.

"He... he doesn't seem like someone who trusts easily," she continued. "Like yourself." She gave Brock a pointed look and a smile tinged with motherly reprimand that drew a small smile from him in return.

"We... bring out good things in each other," Brock admitted, not even having to force the words for how true they were. His heart ached again at the thought of Awen leaving. He had given Brock the most amazing weekend and resolved something with his mother he had never believed would be possible. He didn't ever want to let this whirlwind force of a boy go.

"You never said anything," Brock found himself saying.

"No. I thought it was for you to tell me. I never wanted you to feel it was something you had to share if you didn't want to. I hoped you'd know that I'd support you."

Brock raised a brow at that. "I didn't know," he replied quietly. "Mother, your entire family disowned Aunt Brigid for marrying an Unseelie."

"Yes. I am ashamed to admit it. I tried to reconcile, but she wouldn't have it. Not that I blame her. I have no excuse. I was swayed by my parents' fear during the war, too blinded by it to see how happy she was. And then it was too late to mend that bridge," she said sadly.

Brock smiled softly at her, trying to convey his own forgiveness since he wasn't quite able to say it aloud.

At that moment, Awen arrived back at the table. He looked bright, and though Brock could tell he was making the effort to do so, his smile was genuine when he turned to Mrs Trevanion.

"You know, I was raised by humans in a boarding school, and some of them were very cruel," Awen started, a slight smile on his face as he continued with a conspiratorial tone. "They were always scared I would use my pixie magic on them. Perhaps after dinner, we can visit the school and lure them out into a pixie ring."

Mrs Trevanion laughed in delight and clapped her hands together. "Oh, you are a terrible boy, I knew you couldn't be as perfect as you seemed. I heard pixies could be such pranksters." She continued to chuckle but then looked thoughtful. "Although, I dare say my son could stand to see someone who mistreated you come into some bad luck. So perhaps it is a good match."

Brock laughed and took Awen's hand again, feeling the tremble run through the boy when he did. He was unsure if it was delight or trepidation.

Awen struggled to breathe as Mrs Trevanion hugged him harder than he'd ever been in his life. She practically sobbed next to his ear, "You look after him! And let him look after you too!"

Awen found himself nodding his compliance. A tight lump in his throat at the overwhelming mixture of emotions he felt.

She released him and stepped back to admire

him again, a smile reaching her glistening eyes. "I just wish I had something... Wait!"

Mrs Trevanion pulled back the sleeve of her blouse to reveal a beautiful pearl bracelet. She unclasped it, held it to her chest for a moment and then, with a sigh, pressed it into his hand. "Rocky's father gave me this a long time ago. It was part of a matching set, but the necklace snapped, and the earrings are long gone," she chuckled. "I want you to have it. It isn't much as Christmas gifts go, but it matches your outfit as well as it ever matched any of mine."

"I—I can't!" Awen tried to give it back to her, but she closed his hand over it with a dismissive shake of her head.

"You can. You will. I have plenty of jewellery, I don't have plenty of you. The happiness you clearly bring my son..." She sighed. "You are more precious than any jewellery."

Before he could help himself, Awen flung his arms around her and sobbed noisily against her shoulder as she chuckled and rubbed his back soothingly. He had never felt love like that before, and just being around it was overwhelming in the best of ways.

"There, there. You'll have me crying... again." Mrs Trevanion sniffed.

Awen laughed as he pulled back from her and wiped his eyes on the back of his hand. She took the bracelet from his fingers and clasped it around his wrist, smiling in admiration at the sight.

"Are you ready?" Brock was suddenly behind them with his mother's overnight bag in hand.

She nodded. "You take care, darling Awen, and I hope we'll see each other again very soon." She cupped his face and then turned her enormous smile on Brock before setting off for the door.

❄

When Brock returned from walking his mother to the train station, Awen was sitting on the sofa reading once more.

Brock smiled fondly at the sight.

"Perhaps I should let you borrow some of those?" It was a meaningful offer now that he understood why Awen knew so little about the history of their people.

Awen's brow creased into something like concern. "Can... Can I come here and read them?"

Brock felt a smile spread across his face beyond any control that he had. "Of course. You're always welcome."

Please don't leave.

Awen nodded gratefully and then placed the book down on the pile, avoiding Brock's eyes the whole time. "I... I guess I should go now."

As he stood, Brock grabbed his hand. "Wait... I..." He pulled Awen towards him and held him close to his chest, wanting to memorise the feel of the boy. His now-relieved fear of his mother's acceptance was replaced by the thought of never seeing Awen again despite everything they'd both said and done. What if he left and never came back? What if this was all too much, and he changed his name and disappeared again? What if, one day,

Awen did lose control and no one was there to help him or to stop the Seelie Court taking him? A million scenarios ran through Brock's mind, so many of them extremely unlikely, but all the same, they gave him reason after reason for Awen to stay.

"You don't need to pretend now she's gone," Awen mumbled against him and then let out a shaky breath. "I'm so sorry I did that. I had no right to out you to her like that."

Brock frowned, only holding Awen tighter. Realisation dawned slowly, and he understood what Awen was apologising for. "Awen." Brock breathed his name and then pulled back enough to look at him. "I was the one who said you were my boyfriend."

"I should have stayed in your room—" Awen interjected, but Brock cut him off with a shake of his head.

"And I could have talked my way out of it."

"Even when I linked our arms together?" Awen pushed.

"It doesn't matter," Brock insisted, feeling keenly that Awen was simply trying to find reasons for Brock to reject him. "Either way, I can't regret it. I can't be mad at you for it or at myself. Even if she had walked out and hated me, at least I would have known, and I would finally be myself. And... it was only a little lie."

He repeated Awen's words back to him, still not completely sure what the lie was. But hoping. Oh, so dearly hoping.

"How will you tell her?" Awen cast his eyes down. "I really like her, and I hate to hurt her, but you should tell her the truth. That we aren't together. That this was all fake."

Brock felt Awen's need for him to be strong in that moment, despite the fact that his heart was crumbling. "Awen, this is real for me. I haven't faked one part of today, of how much I've enjoyed your company, the affection I feel for you. Was it fake for you?"

"No." Awen was caught between a sob and a grin, and even so, Brock could see the troubled darkness in his eyes. He was never going to trust easily. "But this was just pretend."

"Then let's go on pretending. Until next Christmas. And the one after. Let's just keep pretending," Brock babbled.

Awen chuckled. "You're ridiculous—"

Before he could finish, Brock pulled him close and kissed him deeply. It was slow but hard as Brock tasted Awen, hungry for him as he pulled their bodies as close together as possible. That closeness only served to remind him of what it felt like to be inside Awen. And perhaps Awen had the same thought as he groaned into Brock's mouth and snaked his arms around his neck. Brock slipped his hand as far up the back of the t-shirt as he could until it was squeezed under the makeshift belt.

With the friction of flesh on flesh, tiny blue sparks crackled between them.

"Is this fake?" Brock broke long enough to mutter against Awen's ear. "Say I'm yours, and it won't be fake. Trust me enough to be mine, and I'll be yours."

Awen whimpered against him, worrying his

lower lip as Brock started to nuzzle into his neck. Brock worked his hand free again and used both hands to untie the scarf and shuck down Awen's oversized pants. Naked beneath, Awen was hard against him. And Brock didn't care if Awen ruined every pair of trousers he owned as long as he stayed with him.

He cupped Awen's balls, which drew a gasp. He fondled them gently in one hand as the other went back around his waist. "You have consumed me since the moment I laid eyes on you. If you want to make me a liar, so be it. If you want this all to have been a game, that's fine, but I know you feel it too. Don't you?"

"The magic?" Awen gasped, breathless and shaking.

Brock shook his head. "Not the magic, the connection."

Tears ran down Awen's face as he smiled through the bliss of Brock's hand moving to stroke his cock.

"This is real," Brock insisted as a blue shimmer wound between them.

"Yes," Awen sobbed, a strangely happy and freeing sound. "Yes, you're mine, I'm yours."

Brock felt like he was engulfed in pure magic moving through him, into him and threatening to burst from his chest in a pounding heartbeat. It zinged over his flesh and crackled between them, and yet it was nothing compared to the connection they had.

Brock did the only thing he could think of in that moment to show his gratitude and affection. His hope for them and his continued plan to worship Awen in any way he could.

He sank to his knees before the boy.

As he brought Awen to climax with his mouth, Brock started to wonder if maybe he shouldn't be a little terrified of Awen after all? He was clearly very dangerous, for he had brought Brock to his knees. He'd already destroyed and rebuilt Brock's life in the space of three days.

Imagine what he might do in a lifetime of little lies.

ABOUT THE AUTHOR

Max Turner is a gay transgender man based in the United Kingdom. He writes speculative and science fiction, fantasy, horror, furry fiction and LGBTQ+ romance and erotica, and more often than not, combinations thereof.

For more about Max and his other publications visit: www.maxturneruk.com

Printed in Great Britain
by Amazon

28158087R10050